P9-DWS-595

JUN – 2014

CALGARY PUBLIC LIBRARY

JUN – 2014

the frog who lost his underpants

JULIETTE MacIVER

ILLUSTRATED BY
Cat Chapman

CANDLEWICK PRESS

Walking through the jungle,
left foot, right foot.
Kicking up the lakka leaves,
making up a song.

Walking through the jungle,
one step, two step,
goes the teddy bear when
who should come along?

Orange-spotted
jungle frog!

Hopping through the jungle,
left hop, right hop.
Looking in the lakka leaves,
scattering the ants.

Hopping through the jungle—
"Help me! Help me!
What became of dignity?
They stole my underpants!"

"Someone stole your underpants?"
Teddy hides a smile.
"Who would steal your undies?
It's hardly worth their while."

"Every frog would give its legs
to own a pair like these.
If mine are lost, I'll die!" says Frog,
sinking to his knees.

Searching in the jungle,
left turn, right turn.
Seeking froggy underpants,
hunting high and low.

Searching in the jungle,
onward, upward.
Climbing up the trees when
who should say hello?

Little chimpanzee!

"Chimpanzee," Teddy says.
"I wonder if you'd mind
helping find Frog's underpants.
See his bare behind?"

"A jungle frog in underpants!
That's something I must see.
We'll find those jolly underpants.
Leave it all to me."

Swinging through the jungle,
left arm, right arm.
Whooshing through the branches,
swooshing out of sight.

Swinging through the jungle,
upside, downside.
Flying through the air when
who should stop their flight?

Big gray elephant!

"Sorry, Mr. Elephant,"
mumbles Teddy Bear.
"We're looking for some underpants;
Frog has lost a pair."

"How dreadful!" cries the elephant.
"Now, please don't think me rude,
    but I am *shocked* to see a frog
    so plainly in the nude."

Swaying through the jungle,
left sway, right sway.
Trampling all the lakka leaves,
rattling every tree.

Swaying through the jungle,
this way, that way.
Seeking Froggy's underpants
when who should Froggy see?

A hundred spotted
jungle frogs!

Fighting in the jungle,
big ones, small ones.
Squabbling in the lakka leaves,
squashing all the ants.

What's that in the midst of them?
Catch them, snatch them.
Frog detects a flash of red . . .

froggy underpants!

Frog is looking stricken;
he turns a pallid green.
"This has to be the worst thing
that I have ever seen."

But Elephant is angry;
he trumpets mighty loud.
All the fighting stops at once,
and Teddy scolds the crowd.

"How *could* you take his undies?
Frog is so distraught!"
The frogs all mutter, "Sorry,"
then Teddy has a thought.

Sewing in the jungle,
this stitch, that stitch.
Making use of lakka leaves,
shaking loose the ants.

Holding them, folding them,
sew them, show them.
Soon they've made a hundred pairs
of froggy underpants.

"But now I'm nothing special,"
says Froggy with a sigh.
"I was the frog in underpants,
but now, well, who am I?"

"I have it!" Frog declares.
"Just watch this clever stunt.
I'll be the only jungle frog
who wears them back to front."

"My froggy friend," Teddy says,
"in underpants or not,
you'll always be a special frog
to me . . . no matter what."

For my darling mother, who's always
been a special frog to me
J. M.

For trusty comrades, Stella and Holly
C. C.

Text copyright © 2013 by Juliette MacIver
Illustrations copyright © 2013 by Cat Chapman

All rights reserved. No part of this book may be reproduced, transmitted,
or stored in an information retrieval system in any form or by any means,
graphic, electronic, or mechanical, including photocopying, taping, and
recording, without prior written permission from the publisher.

First U.S. edition 2014

Library of Congress Catalog Card Number 2013944130
ISBN 978-0-7636-6782-5

14 15 16 17 18 19 SCP 10 9 8 7 6 5 4 3 2 1

Printed in Humen, Dongguan, China

This book was typeset in Gill Sans Light.
The illustrations were done in watercolor and ink.

Candlewick Press
99 Dover Street
Somerville, Massachusetts 02144

visit us at www.candlewick.com